Haunted
Houses
on
Halloween

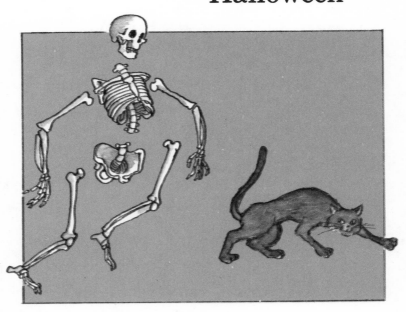

Haunted Houses on Halloween

By Lillie Patterson

Drawings by Doug Cushman

GARRARD PUBLISHING COMPANY
CHAMPAIGN, ILLINOIS

To
William Henry Patterson

Library of Congress Cataloging in Publication Data

Patterson, Lillie.
   Haunted houses on Halloween.

   (First holiday books)
   SUMMARY: Retells two folktales in which a young man
becomes involved with a ghost and a clever hunter meets
a mysterious cat.
   1. Tales. [1. Folklore. 2. Ghost stories]
I. Cushman, Doug. II. Title. III. Series.
PZ8.1.P232Ha   [398.2] [E]   78-11382
ISBN 0-8116-7253-0

The Skeleton's Secret

Ivan set out to seek his fortune.

One night in the late fall,

he walked along a road

in the cold rain.

The lad had no money,

and his clothes were ragged.

He was very hungry.

Through the mist and rain,
he saw a big farmhouse.
Ivan went up to the door
and knocked on it.
A man opened the door.
"Good evening," he said.
"Why are you out
on a night like this?"
"I am wet and tired,"
Ivan said.
"Would you let me
sleep here for the night?
In return,
I will work for you tomorrow."
"I'm sorry," the man answered,
"but tonight I have guests.
There are no empty beds."

"Thank you anyway,"
Ivan said in a sad voice.
He turned to leave,
but the man called him back.
"I have another house
in the woods nearby.
You may stay there.
I must warn you, though.
It is not a safe place
to stay."
"I would welcome any place,"
Ivan answered.
"It is a pretty little house,"
said the man.
"My servants use it
during the day.
But no one stays there after dark."

"Why not?" asked Ivan.

The stranger answered

in a low voice,

"The house is haunted!"

Ivan laughed.

"Well," he said,

"ghosts won't bother me.

I will be glad

to sleep in the haunted house."

So the man gave Ivan

a basket of food

for his supper.

Ivan took the basket

and walked down a dark road.

Before long

he found the house

deep in the woods.

Ivan started a fire
in the fireplace.
The warm glow from the fire
made the little house
a cheerful place.

Ivan took off his wet coat
and sat down
in front of the fire.
Then he opened
the basket of food.
The man had given him
fresh bread, cold meat,
a big piece of cheese,
and a jug of rich milk.
Before he ate,
Ivan put some bread crumbs
in his pockets.
"Bread crumbs keep ghosts away,"
he told himself.
Next,
he turned his jacket inside out.
And he put his knife nearby.

"That should be enough
to keep any ghost away,"
he said.
Then Ivan began to eat supper.

Suddenly
he heard a loud noise
far up in the chimney.
"I'm coming down!"
"Aha!"
Ivan called up the chimney.
"Come on down, then.
But don't keep me
from eating my supper."

Plop!
Down the chimney
fell the big,
bony leg of a man.
It hopped over the hot coals
and stood in the middle
of the room.
Ivan went on eating.

Soon a voice
called down the chimney
a second time.
"I'm coming down!"
"Come on down, then."
Ivan started to eat
another piece of bread.
Plip, plop!
Down came a second leg.
It hopped over the hot coals
and stood near the first leg.

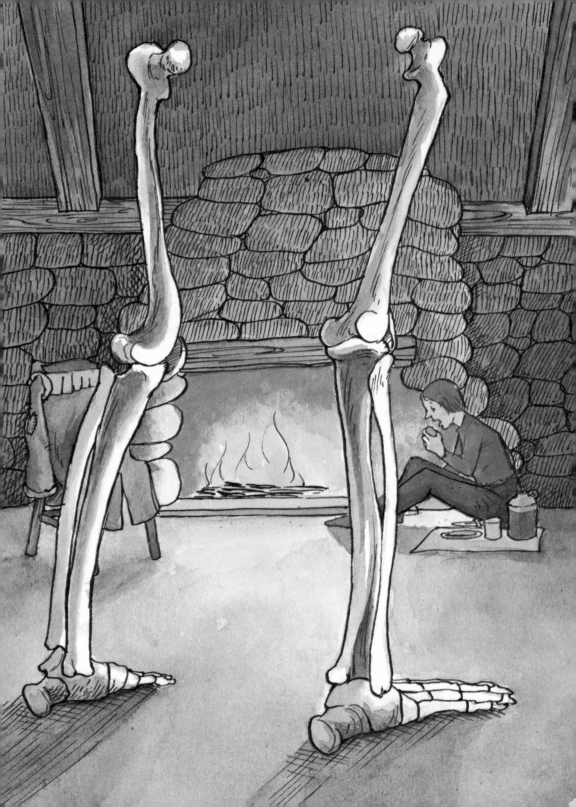

The hungry lad
put another piece of cheese
into his mouth.
"I'm coming down.
I'm coming down!"
the voice called again.
"Come on down, then,"
Ivan answered.
Plippety-plop-plop!
Down fell the body
of a man.
It rolled
over the hot coals
and across the floor.
Up it went
on top of the two bony legs.
Ivan looked at it hard.

Then he put
some cheese and meat
between two pieces of bread.
"I'm coming down!"
the voice called,
louder than before.
Plippety-plop, plippety-plop!
Down fell two long arms.
They jumped over the coals
and skipped across the floor.
Soon
they were on the shoulders
of the body.
The body was finished
except for the head.
Then the voice called out
one last time.

"I'm coming down.
I'm coming down!"
"Come down
and be done with it,"
called Ivan.
He finished eating
the last bit of bread.
Plippety-plop,
plippety-plop-plop!
Down the chimney
came a big head.

It rolled over the coals
and across the floor
and landed on the body.
The skeleton
was now finished.
Ivan drank
the last drop of milk.

Then he turned
to his skeleton guest.
"So you have been
haunting this house,"
he said.
"What do you want?"
"You are not afraid of me?"
asked the strange visitor.
"No, I am not afraid of you,"
said Ivan.
"But I am tired. I came here
for a good night's sleep.
Why do you haunt
this pretty little house?"
"Follow me,
and I will tell you,"
said the skeleton.

Bold Ivan
followed the skeleton.
It led him down the steps
and into the cellar
of the little house.

There, the skeleton pointed
with a bony finger
to a stone on the floor.
"Lift the stone," he said.
Ivan pulled hard
and lifted the stone.
"Oh, my goodness!" he cried.
"What a treasure!"
Under the stone
lay a big box filled with gold.

"Now I will tell you a story,"
said the skeleton.
"I have waited many years
for someone to come
who was not afraid of me.
I needed someone bold enough
to stay in the house
while my body was put together.

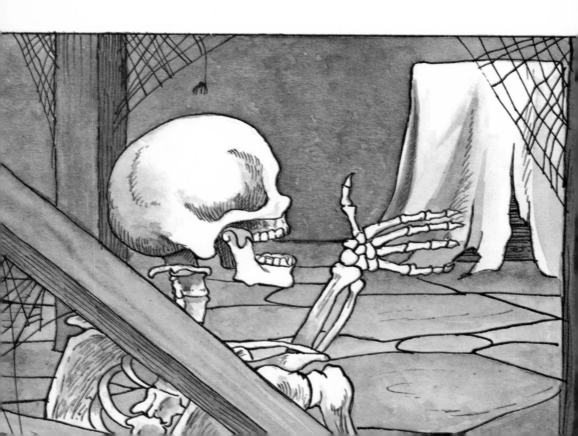

You must now help me
to right a great wrong."
"How can I help you?"
Ivan asked.
"I once lived in this house,"
the skeleton began.
"The kind man who owns it
was my friend.

But I cheated him
out of a lot of money.
Tomorrow you must give half
of this gold to him.
The other half
you may keep for yourself.
If you do not do this,
I will come back to haunt you."
For once,
Ivan did not know
what to say.
Finally he spoke.
"I will do as you wish,"
he promised the skeleton.
"Thank you," said the visitor.
"Now I can rest in peace."
Poof!

The skeleton disappeared
into the air.

Early the next morning
the man who owned the house
came to the woods.
He thought he would find
a frightened guest.
He was very surprised
when he heard the story
of what had happened.
Ivan gave the man
half of the gold.
In thanks,
the man gave him
the little house to live in.
The two became good friends.
In time,
Ivan married a pretty girl
who lived in the village.

He settled down
and became a rich farmer.
As for the skeleton,
he rested in peace
and was never heard of again.

Black Cat, Witch Cat

Late one Halloween afternoon
a hunter was caught
in a storm.
The woods became
as dark as night.
Thunder shook the mountains,
and rain poured down.
The hunter
ran through the woods.
His two hunting dogs
followed close behind him.

"Hurry up!"
the man called to his dogs.
"We must find
a place to stay
until the storm is over."
After a time
they came to a small house
deep in the woods.
The house was empty,
so the hunter went in.
He lit a fire
in the fireplace
and took off
his wet coat.
After he had sat
by the fire for a while,
he was warm and dry.

His two big dogs
lay on the floor beside him.
The October wind howled outside
and rattled the windows.
Raindrops poured down
upon the roof.
"I am glad
we are safe inside,"
the hunter told his dogs.
Suddenly
the dogs growled.
"What is that?"
the hunter wondered.
Scratch! Scratch!
Something was outside
the front door.
Scratch! Scratch!

The noise grew louder.
The two dogs
jumped to their feet.
"Quiet,"
the hunter said to them.
He sat in his chair
listening for another sound.
The scratching noise came again.
This time
it was followed
by a sad cry.
"Miaouw, miaouw."
The latch
on the front door lifted.
C-r-e-a-k! C-r-e-a-k!
Slowly, slowly,
the door opened.

A big black cat
leaped into the room.
It was shaking
from the cold.
Water dripped
from its wet fur.
The cat jumped onto a table
in the middle of the room.

The dogs growled and snapped,
ready to bite.
But before the dogs
could bite the cat,
it began to speak.
"Great Hunter-of-the-Hills!"
cried the cat.
"Please help me.

I am so wet,

so cold, and so hungry.

Please hold back your dogs

and save my life."

"Down, boys!"

the hunter told his dogs.

He turned

to the talking cat.

"Come and sit by the fire.

I will not let

my dogs hurt you."

The hunter told his dogs

to lie down.

The dogs did

as they were told.

But their eyes

never left the cat.

Deep growls
came from their throats.
The hair
on their backs stood up.
"Good Hunter,
I cannot come close
to the fire,"
the cat said.
"I am still afraid
of your big dogs.
Please tie them up."
"My dogs
will not hurt you,"
the hunter said again.
"Besides,
I have nothing
with which to tie them."

"I have something you can use,"
purred the cat.
"Here, use this strong hair."
The black cat held out
a long, dark piece of hair.
By this time, the hunter
was thinking fast.
"This is a strange cat,"
he thought to himself.
The hunter turned his back
to the cat.
He made the cat think
that he was tying up the dogs.
Instead,
he tied both ends of the hair
around a big piece of wood
near the fireplace.

When the cat
thought that the dogs were tied,
it jumped down from the table.
It went closer to the fire.
The creature sat down
to dry its fur.
The cat watched the hunter.

The two dogs
watched the cat.
And the hunter
watched all three of them.
Suddenly
he saw that the cat
was growing bigger.
"What is happening, cat?"
cried the hunter.
"You are growing bigger
by the minute."
"It is just my hair,"
purred the cat.
"When my hair dries,
my fur stands out.
That is why
I look bigger to you."

The hunter
kept watching the cat.
It was growing
bigger and bigger.
The hunter was now sure
that the cat was evil.
"You don't fool me,"
said the hunter.

"You are now as big
as a small cow."
"Do not fear, Great Hunter,"
answered the black cat.
"When my skin begins to dry,
it makes me look bigger."
The hunter
did not take his eyes
from the cat.
The dogs kept on growling.
All the while
the cat got bigger—
and bigger.
"Begone, you wicked cat!"
the hunter called out.
"You must be an evil demon
in the shape of a cat.

You have grown
as tall as the door!"
At these words
the black cat
lifted its back.
It was so big
that its hair
almost touched the ceiling.
Suddenly,
it gave a loud screech
and changed
into a big black witch.
"Your time has come,
Great Hunter,"
hissed the witch.
"Your dogs are tied
and cannot help you.

Tighten hair!"
the witch shrieked. "Tighten!"
The hair did not tighten
around the dogs,
as the witch thought it would.
Instead,
it closed around the wood
and cut it in two.
"Up, boys!"
the hunter called to his dogs.
"Help me!"
The hounds jumped up,
ready to help the hunter.
They set their sharp teeth
in the witch's bony legs.
The witch kicked
and scratched and yowled.

But the dogs held on.
Suddenly the demon gave
a wild cry of rage.
E-e-e-e-e-k!
The next minute the witch
turned into a big puff of smoke
and disappeared up the chimney.
So the hunter
and his dogs
slept without fear
that Halloween night
in the haunted house.